GUILD
OF THE
BEACH RATS

2022, TWB Press
www.twbpress.com

Dedication

In loving memory, to my first ever beta readers, Mom & Dad.

Guild of the Beach Rats
Copyright © 2022 by Michael J.P. Whitmer

Edited by Terry Wright

Cover Art by Terry Wright

ISBN: 978-1-944045-94-4

Guabancex

(Gwa-bahn-she)

Centuries ago, across the Florida peninsula and around the Caribbean, the indigenous tribes believed *Guabancex* to be the destructive side of Mother Nature. Her volatile temper could wipe the land clean with the sweep of Her hand. She was known as the Goddess of the Wind, the Mother of Storms, and the Destroyer of Everything. Those who have seen Her wrath say She is not to be trifled with. Pity the souls in this story who did not heed that warning.

Chapter One - Reanimation

Max's skeletal remains dislodged from the ocean bed. Crustaceans and barnacles clung to the bones where they had found refuge on his long-sunken corpse. He floated for a moment, still as death, while the ocean's tide and a supernatural force, moving like a song, pulled him in opposing directions. The ocean lost to the force, and his remains rose toward the moon's glow blanketing the surface.

His bones shed their parasitic crustaceans. Ligaments, muscles, and skin grew while veins and arteries threaded throughout. As his body reanimated, so too did his mind and senses, and musical notes in his skull lured him back to life. However, the supernatural force blocked access to his memories. His past history would be shrouded in fog and confusion.

Rise, the voice demanded in his mind. *Rise.*

On the crest of a wave, Max washed ashore, and the breakers rolled him in the sand until he finally stuck in the shallows. Internal flesh and organs seeded themselves and grew to appear functional, and his mottled cheeks reddened with newly restored blood flow, though his heartbeat was nonexistent. As he gasped his first breath, his eyes leaked out the last of the ocean's salt water.

The ethereal song that woke him from his watery slumber drifted from a dark figure perched on the dune. The cloaked-one held an outstretched hand to Max.

The Master was calling.

A gang of children stood along either side of the cloaked Master. They were of various ages, one boy with a peach-fuzz mustache looked old enough to drive. He sported a buzzed-bald head, except for one dreadlock shaped like a rat's tail in the back. The others were just past the stage of wetting the bed. Many had no shirts or shoes. Those who did were dressed in ragged tank tops, torn swimsuits, and flip flops.

Max clawed his way out of the surf.

Five children scampered down the dune and rushed to Max's side. One girl with shaggy hair and brown eyes as bright as a new day in spring draped a blanket over his body.

Her visage tugged at a dead space in his memory.

Who is she? Why does she look so familiar?

The other children helped him stand then gently ushered him closer to the cloaked figure. Under the glow of moonlight, Max could see the man's build was long and lean like a swimmer's. His stringy white hair protruded wildly from under a bandana, and a gray beard hid most of his face. He wore a leather highwayman's coat, open enough to see his bare chest and a strange necklace with a fragmented jewel, in the shape of an eye, hanging from his sinewy neck. He had tucked a sheathed knife behind a sash that held up his frayed trousers.

Max fell to his knees before his master. "What's happening?" Max uttered up to him.

"Have no fear, my child." His voice was calmer than the ocean after a storm. "I have brought you back from the sea to walk amongst the living again."

"Why?"

"My city has lost its voice. Give the people something to sing about. Set them free from their oppressors and bring live music back to the beaches."

Max bowed to his master's command while a name echoed in his foggy mind.

Bright-Eyes.

Chapter Two - Homecoming

Morgan Roth stared out the Greyhound bus's window at her childhood home town. Decaying and vacant buildings clung to the shore where a proud and quaint coastal cityscape once stood. A young child inhabitant with an apathetic face stood on the sidewalk and stared at a homeless citizen digging in a trash barrel. The mangy person was so layered in rags, its gender and age Morgan could not grasp.

Places of worship were boarded up, and their marquee signs and crosses were covered with black sheets. These veils were embroidered with an emblem of a coiled serpent in the eye of a hurricane. Upon further inspection, she realized the eye was a woman's eye, and the serpent's body represented her whirling locks of hair. The emblem showed up painted on tenement and store fronts, and as decals on the back of pickup trucks, minivans, and smoking clunkers that could barely make it down the road. The influence of *The Fellowship of Her Lady by the Sea* had reached into every tier of society.

Morgan had heard of the cult from her friend, the editor of Masque Media, Blaire Hudson. She focused on social issues of the day, and since the Fellowship banned newspapers, she continued her reporting on her blog. Blaire would be waiting for her at the bus station.

The bus stopped at a red light. On the corner stood three young people dressed in white with black cloth bands tied on their upper arms. They waved and offered out a pamphlet to a passerby who didn't make eye contact, simply accepted the religious propaganda and moved on.

"We are always watching," one of them called out to Morgan, looking down from the bus.

She quickly sat back and stared straight forward, her nerves a bit rattled from the perceived threat.

The light changed to green.

Morgan was the only passenger, which made exiting the bus easy.

The driver spoke for the first time in hundreds of miles. "If I were you, I wouldn't linger around here after dark."

"I don't scare easily, mister," she lied.

"Famous last words." The driver closed the door and goosed the throttle down the lane to *Passenger*

Pickup.

The station was empty, aside from a bearded café worker and a couple of decommissioned busses with flat tires and broken windows. Across the street, on the side of a withered apartment building, the Fellowship's symbol was painted over other graffiti.

She ordered an overpriced latte from the café.

"What brings you to town?" the barista asked as he began to prepare her order.

"I grew up here... Also, work. Masque Media. Have you heard of it?"

The barista nodded. "Fake news, they say."

Morgan frowned. "Are you from around here?"

"God no. I'm just passing through from Miami. Ran out of money. My partner and I get too many stares

Michael J.P. Whitmer

here, being we're gay, and all. We're saving to move on to the west coast."

Intolerance had always been an issue in this town, all the way back to its founders. Hearing about it now, she wanted to apologize for the entire population. "This place has changed a lot in other ways, from what I've heard."

He poured the espresso. "Yeah, you're not wrong. People have turned up missing. You should try to be indoors by nightfall." He had lowered his voice, as if told by management not to talk about the disappearances with customers.

"Thanks. I've a ride on the way." For making a decent coffee, Morgan tipped him a dollar.

Sitting at a curbside café table, she sipped her drink and called Blaire on her cell phone. She should have arrived by now.

No answer and her voicemail box was full.

Blaire, what's the holdup. Is everything okay? she texted and punched the send button.

Morgan wasn't worried. She had a few hours before dark. The café worker was cleaning up. The bus driver had already made his getaway. She didn't feel comfortable hanging out downtown, especially alone.

Her phone chimed in a text from Blaire. *Sorry. It's unsafe for me to go out. Meet me at the studio.*

Morgan scowled. She was pissed but more ashamed that ordering an Uber would bring her bank account close to zero. She phoned for a ride and decided she would need an advance on her first paycheck from Blaire.

The Uber driver showed up just as the bearded café worker closed shop.

The rideshare took the fastest route his GPS recommended, which still required crossing several bridges and the ditch to get to the beaches where she grew up. The ditch was the longest river in the state. It flowed north and meandered through twelve counties, once called the *River May* by the French then renamed the *Río San Juan* by the Spanish.

The more bridges she traversed, the more the Fellowship's presence faded. Church crosses and a Buddhist meditation center on Third Street stood without the black veils. Though Morgan wasn't religious, a cult she wasn't familiar with gave her the willies. She didn't know what kind of weird rituals to expect.

The driver dropped her off in a small strip-mall parking lot on First Street. The building was close enough to the beach that Morgan could hear the waves roll to shore. Masque Media's studio sat between a closed restaurant under renovation and a used furniture store. Across the street, a tall chain-link fence topped with barbed wire surrounded a vacant lot of sand and palm trees. She recalled a charming public library once stood there. A bronze dolphin statue greeted folks, and kids often rode it like a playground horse.

Blaire stood waiting at the studio door. She wore pajamas. Her hair was in a messy bun, and she reeked like she hadn't bathed in a week. As soon as Morgan stepped inside, Blaire closed the door and locked it then peered anxiously out the side glass, scanning the parking lot, the street, and the vacant lot of sand and palm trees. Seemingly satisfied that the area was clear of danger, she turned to Morgan. "Sorry about my paranoid behavior."

"What's going on, Blaire?"

"It's gotten worse since we last emailed each other."

"What's the problem?"

"The Fellowship." She walked past Morgan, motioning her to follow her through the unlit lobby and dark newsroom. White bulletin boards, a projector, printer, and other office equipment that hadn't been operated in months crammed the once bustling media center.

She followed Blaire into a small back office. Paperwork was scattered across the desk. A computer fan made a squealing noise like it hadn't been powered off since the front office had closed down.

Blaire flopped in her desk chair. "I'm so glad you made it. As you can see, I'm in dire need of a journalist. It's unfortunate about your last article going bust. A bad source could happen to anyone."

Morgan sat on the edge of the desk. "The mayor flat-out lied to me." Her last publisher 'let her go' for heralding false information about the NYPD. "The paper said they didn't need me anymore."

"Well, I need you. This damned city needs you."

Morgan spotted a sleeping bag and blankets on the floor. "Are you living here, Blaire?"

Her face reddened with ire. "My apartment is being watched by the Fellowship."

Morgan didn't fully grasp the gravity of such espionage, but the fear on her friend's face appeared real. "Why are they watching you?"

"I'm onto them. I received a video recording from an anonymous source, supposedly of one of their cult rituals.

Plus, I blogged a rebuke about them, how they're using black magic to take over the city. They're not very happy with me."

"What was on the recording?"

"I don't know. I never got to watch it. It's on a thumb drive that someone slipped me. When a mob showed up wearing hoods and waving Fellowship banners, I panicked, left a lot behind while getting the hell out of my condo. I've been hiding out here for the past week."

"What about the police? Have you filed a report?"

"The cops couldn't care less. They say the disappearances are a more important waste of their time."

"What do you know about that?"

"I've interviewed families of the missing. They've gone to the cops with their stories, but they've all been dismissed. Adults go missing all the time. I left their testimonies and recordings at my condo. All their accounts are similar, connecting each missing person to the Fellowship before their loved one disappeared. There's some serious corruption going on in this town, and I'm not talking legends about a band of pirates."

Her reference to the folklore surrounding the town's history made Morgan want to chuckle, tales of buccaneers and bushwhackers, but she knew where Blaire was going with this. "Do you want me to retrieve your evidence from your condo?"

"I can't show my face anywhere near there. I'm sorry. My anxiety is off the charts. I'm a scared mess."

A Maltese dog sprang into her lap and started licking her face.

"This is Samson. He's my therapy dog. He's also why so much of my stuff got left behind." Blaire had said the last sentence in a weird baby-voice that intensified Samson's face-licking.

"He's cute, but I'll need more than Samson to break this story."

Samson ceased his slobber-fest and curled up on Blaire's lap.

She opened a drawer and took out an envelope and a list of provisions, which she slid across the cluttered desk toward Morgan. "Here's three hundred dollars and my debit card." She next handed her a set of keys. "The large key is to the condo, and the other fits the studio." Last, Blaire carefully placed a 9mm Glock on the envelope. "It's loaded."

"You think I'll need that?"

"If I'm right about the Fellowship, and they're still scoping out my place, then yes. Plus, you're going over the ditch. You'll need it."

"I've heard it's dangerous to be

out after dark."

"Yeah, just don't get caught."

"Okay." Morgan hated admitting the need for a gun as she tucked it into her handbag. "I'll try to be back by midnight."

"Be careful," Blaire stressed. "The farther from the beaches you get, the more likely you are to become one of the missing. Who knows how long that danger will last, though? Video evidence of cruel rituals, or worse, is what we need to put the Fellowship away." Blaire leaned forward. "So failure is not an option."

Chapter Three - The Band

With a sun-kissed face dotted by freckles, Bright-Eyes scoped out Gill's Hardware store, a redbrick building on Third Street with a huge display window that showcased camping gear and mannequins fishing in a barrel. She was barefoot and wearing a 4XL t-shirt that fit her like a dress. On the front of the shirt in decaying letters read one word: *D-A-R-E.* And she did dare to do anything. Bright-Eyes was afraid of nothing.

The door dinged when she entered. Right away she drew the attention of the few patrons and the two shop owners, brothers Jeremy and Ryan Gill. The group of male customers sported similar style beards and wore cargo shorts and plaid-flannel shirts. They'd gathered by the front counter where a glass case of hunting rifles stood, and gas generators, still in boxes, lined the far wall.

She walked to the nearest aisle and stopped in front of an assortment of drills and tools.

Ryan, the youngest brother, left the counter and poked his head around the corner. "Can I help you with anything?"

She stared at him, mute.

"Are you lost?" The girl's face looked familiar. "Do I know you?"

Bright-Eyes grabbed a Makita drill and bolted for the door.

"Shit. Stop. Thief." Ryan took off after her.

She sprinted down the sidewalk and ducked around the corner of the building. Ryan got to the corner in time to see her crossing four lanes of traffic. She dodged two vehicles while Ryan was nearly flattened by a speeding delivery truck. Doggedly, he caught up with her in an alleyway where he stopped cold. She wasn't alone. Rat-Tail, slingshot at the ready, and two teenaged beach punks wielding their skateboards like bats shielded her.

"Am I supposed to be scared of you Beach Rats? Hand over the drill." He huffed for air but refused the urge to double over.

"Don't die on us, gramps." Rat-Tail laughed.

"They're with me, Ryan." The voice had come from behind him, near the entrance of the alleyway.

Ryan spun around while reaching for the firearm hidden under his shirt, but when he saw the speaker, he didn't draw the weapon. "What the hell?" The sun, sweat, and disbelief at the sight of a familiar face rattled him. "Max?"

Max walked toward him. "Sorry about the antics with the drill. I'm trying to keep a low profile and don't want to be seen in public."

"Max? Holy hell." Ryan hugged him and suddenly pulled away, shocked that Max was cold despite the Florida heat. "Dude, you haven't aged a bit. The Gold Coast must be heaven. We thought you'd never come back to this shit-town. What are you doing here?"

"I'm putting the band back together." Max held out a flyer. In funky lettering it read:

Guild of the Beach Rats

Never Die Concert!

Reunion show, one night only!

Cartoonish rats surrounded the

words, some crawling from a trapdoor in the sand. One rat held a picket-sign: *KEEP OFF DUNES.*

"Cool," Ryan murmured.

"You still play bass?" Max asked him.

"Not since the Fellowship banned concerts on the beach. I still have my guitar, though."

"Get it tuned up. The band's booked to play the Beach Pavilion."

"The old boardwalk stage? That hasn't been used in years, not since the Fellowship busted it up."

"A private promoter is on board," Max said with a grin, as if that explained everything.

"I don't know, maybe. Convincing Jeremy is another story. He's more pissed...you know, since the night of the storm that you disappeared."

"That's why I'm glad Bight-Eyes lured you out here and not Jeremy.

He's always had a bad temper. You're more even keel."

"What happened that night?"

"I still don't know, exactly."

"Dude, I need something from you...some reason to give Jeremy. Did Morgan dump you or something?"

"I think we met that night...after the evacuation orders were issued. I can't remember anything for sure."

"That's it?" Ryan pressed.

Max closed his eyes, hoping that simple act would bring back a thought or a memory. Seeing only a wall of darkness, Max shuddered and didn't think about it further.

"You didn't show for the recording session. Why was surfing the Gold Coast more important than the band?"

"Ryan, I never left."

"What do you mean? I heard—"

"I've been dead for the past ten

years."

Ryan paled. "No way, Dude."

Another beach punk ran into the alley. "They're starting. Hurry."

"Follow us, Ryan. This you gotta see. You'll figure out what we're up against."

Max led the group deeper into the alley. The passageway twisted several times until it opened into a shantytown constructed of junk. Clothes and tarps hung from wire stretched overhead, blocking out the afternoon sun but baking the place in a hot rancid odor.

"The Guild is in real trouble, my friend," Max stated in a hushed tone as they moved between huts and tents scattered helter-skelter. "Our grip on the city is slipping. The Fellowship of Her Lady by the Sea has taken hold."

"Everybody knows that, Max, but

get this. I hear the mayor was elected because of his association with the Fellowship." Now Ryan's voice was a whisper. "The cops are beholding to them, as well."

"It's worse than you think."

Beyond a smelly pile of trash, the group crouched down at a shack that appeared more sturdy and larger than the other makeshift dwellings. Max ushered Ryan, Rat-Tail, Bright-Eyes, and the other teens to a glassless window. "Look."

Inside, a poor family of four gathered around a sand pit dug in the middle of the shack. The father, mother, and sister circled the hole in which the brother stood. As if they were writhing to shed their skin, the family danced and hissed and flicked their tongues at the boy.

"Dad, Mom, I'm scared," the boy cried out with tears streaming down his face. His sister kicked sand on him as she danced and ignored her brother's whining. The family's dance intensified into mania. The boy's eyes rolled back in their sockets, showing all white, and he started to convulse violently.

One of the beach punks watching couldn't resist the urge to help a fellow youth in need. He ducked around Rat-Tail standing guard at the doorway and rushed into the shack. Diving into the sand, he reached a hand down into the pit. "Grab on. I'll save you."

When the boy's eyes rolled forward, angry serpents uncoiled from each socket. The snakes lashed out, sinking black fangs into the punk's hand. The family hissed and whirled as their eyes, too, ejected serpents that struck the punk's face and arms, injecting black acid that would dissolve his flesh into ash. Before the punk could utter a scream, his body transformed to a black residue that bled away into the sand.

Ryan fell back from the window and stumbled into the trash, too shocked and frightened to draw his pistol. The shack was suddenly surrounded by thirty beach punks armed with sticks, bricks, and boards, and they wore rabid expressions on their weathered faces.

Max nodded to Rat-Tail, who pulled a slingshot from his back pocket. The punks charged into the hut and attacked the family of snake-eyed demons. Nobody came out until the hissing had stopped.

Max helped Ryan to his feet and led him out of the shantytown. At a jog in the alleyway, Ryan stopped and leaned against a brick wall, breathing hard and still trembling from what he had witnessed. "What was that all about, Max?"

"The black magic you saw back there is the same sort of power that brought me back from the grave."

Ryan stared at the ground. "I don't understand."

Max stepped to Ryan, and placing his hands over Ryan's temples, shut his eyes and thought back to the night ten years ago.

Some ungodly force closed Ryan's eyes. He saw a tower of darkness and felt a rush of cold water slam over him. He couldn't breathe. He couldn't swim. He was drowning.

Max released him.

He fell to his knees, gasping and shivering. "W-what was that?" His voice trembled with more fear than he'd ever known.

"That's the last thing I remember that night, Ryan."

"You drowned, yet you're here. Are you a ghost?"

"Something more. The Master of the Guild has given me life to restore the town's voice."

"What do you want me to do?"

"Convince Jeremy to pick up his drum sticks again and get ready to play the show of our lives."

***

Ryan, still in a daze, returned to the hardware shop. The patrons had cleared out. He placed the drill back on the shelf.

"What happened?" Jeremy asked, walking into the aisle.

"She ditched the drill, so I got it back. Did you call the cops?" Ryan didn't make eye contact with his brother.

"It's been an hour and still nobody in blue showed up. Where are my tax dollars going? At least you got the product back." Jeremy noticed Ryan nervously rub his neck. "What's wrong?"

"There's something else." Ryan handed him the flyer and watched Jeremy's nostalgic glimmer as he stared at the band's advertisement. For a fleeting moment, the prospect of playing again sparked an old passion in him, and then the glimmer evaporated. "What's this shit?"

Max stepped into the aisle behind Ryan. "We need you back in the band."

"Max?" Jeremy paled as if he'd seen a ghost. He pointed a stiff index finger at him. "You got a lot of nerve comin' back here."

Ryan jumped in. "Give him a chance to explain, Jeremy."

"You're falling for this crap? A concert on the beach?" He crumpled the flyer and tossed it at Ryan.

"You're a fool, man."

Max stepped forward. "It has to happen, with or without your drums, Jeremy."

"Yeah? We said the same thing ten years ago when your ass bailed on the recording session. We don't need your stinkin' keyboard. We don't need no lead singer. Without as much as a fuck-you very much or a simple goodbye, you surfed off into the sunset. After everything my family did for you?"

"Easy, Jeremy," Ryan put in.

"Where was he when our dad died? Where were you, Max? He took you in, damnit, and you blow off his funeral? You're an ass."

"I didn't know—"

"Damn you, Max."

"Jeremy, you're out of line. Let him explain. Dad would want us to play in the band again. When's the last time this town had live music on the beach? Besides, it's only one show. You can play your drums again."

"That dream died with the damn Fellowship, Ryan."

"Replaced with what? Hoping for the big hurricane to hit so you can sell generators to our neighbors who can't afford them? Dad would be ashamed."

"If you're too good for this store, then go." Jeremy advanced on Ryan with his fists clinched.

Ryan backed away before Jeremy could get within swinging distance then turned and nudged Max to the exit. "He's going to need time to cool off," Ryan uttered.

Max got in the last word. "When you change your mind, Jeremy, you can find us at the old practice spot."

Jeremy slammed the door behind

them.

"He hasn't changed much." Max shrugged. "I bet he can still thrash on those drums."

Ryan nodded. "If he had been with us in the alleyway and saw what happened in the shack, he would be joining us now."

Max looked up and down the street and scowled at all the Fellowship banners and signs. "I just hope we can generate enough good vibes to save the city."

Chapter Four - The Condo

The *Plaza Condominium and Marina* was supposed to be the coast's premier riverfront complex. The 22-story, 209-unit high-rise had all the amenities: Olympic swimming pools, rooftop tennis courts, and sundeck gardens. However, after years of mismanagement and an ongoing labor dispute with the union, the Mediterranean architecture and lush landscaping now sat in spoil. Blaire's condo was on the tenth floor.

Morgan rode the elevator up.

The door to Blaire's unit had been forced open, leaving the lock and frame broken and splintered. Morgan stood in the doorway and stared into the dark interior. She tried the light switch on the wall.

Click. Click. Nothing.

Fear prickled her neck hairs. The power was out, which was why Blaire's list of provisions included a flashlight.

Morgan reached into her bag, nudged the pistol aside, and pulled out the flashlight. After pressing the button, a cone of light illuminated the foyer.

She moved into the darkness, wielding the six-foot beam. Blaire had told her that the flash data-drives, recordings, and documents were in a box by her bedroom door. Clothes and some of Samson's things would be draped over it. She hadn't had time to grab it all on her way out.

Morgan wagged the flashlight, casting the beam across the living room and kitchen. Both rooms had been ransacked. She walked on utensils scattered about and kicked a can of food across the floor. Stepping over cushions from flipped furniture, she found Blaire's bedroom at the other end of the room and aimed the light to where the box should have been. Nothing but some towels and Samson's squeaky toy bone, which she bent down and retrieved then stuffed into her bag. She poked the flashlight's beam into the corners and even checked under the bed. No box of flash data-drives, recordings, or documents revealed itself. She headed for the closet, but when she heard utensils clattering beneath someone's footsteps, she paused. "Who's there?"

No answer, only the sounds of shuffling feet in the other room.

Fighting panic, she stepped to the bedroom doorway and swept the cone of light around the living room. A hooded figure in a black robe stood near the foyer. The light couldn't penetrate the shadow of the hood, but it revealed dark pits where the figure's eyes and mouth were supposed to be.

Her heart started gaining speed like a ball rolling downhill. "This is my friend's place," she called out. "I have a key." She reached for the pistol in her bag.

The hooded figure hissed at her, and snakes whipped out of the eye pits in its dark face.

Morgan spun out of the way and ducked behind the bedroom wall. The fangs barely missed her arm, and then the snakes retreated into the hood. When she spun back to the doorway with the gun drawn, the figure and his snake-eyes were gone. Fearing the serpents might lash out at her from the shadows, she held her ground, and as her hands shook, she pointed the light and gun all around the room. Seeing nothing, she stalked to the foyer and stopped to look out the door.

The robed figure was posted at the end of the hall, hissing. She fired a warning shot in his direction then bolted toward the elevator doors. Two serpents came out of nowhere and struck at her with open jaws, their black fangs just missing her as she rounded the corner to the elevator enclave.

"Drop the weapon, ma'am." An officer in blue blocked her way to the elevator, gun drawn and aimed at her.

She dropped the Glock, stepped back, and raised her hands. "There's a creepy guy after me." Panic laced her voice as she glanced behind her.

"Calm down, ma'am." He lowered his weapon. "A tenant phoned in about a disturbance on this floor."

"They're behind me, down the hallway." She sidestepped him to distance herself from the serpents, expecting them to attack her again, at any moment.

"Wait by the elevator." The cop advanced toward the corner, his gun at the ready then peered into the hallway. "It's clear."

"They were there."

"Let's get you downstairs. I'll come back later and look around." He marched toward the elevator, only stopping long enough to pick up Morgan's gun.

She didn't take her eyes off the corner, expecting the snakes to materialize again. Once on the elevator and four floors down, she felt a little more at ease. "Thank God the cops got here."

"I'm the building security officer, ma'am. I'd like to know what you were doing running around the hallway with a gun."

Damn, he's not even a real cop.

"I was checking on my friend's condo. It was broken into. Where were you for that burglary, mister security officer?"

"You're friends with Blaire?"

"Yes."

"Are you a godless bitch, too?"

"Excuse me?"

"The Fellowship is trying to restore this city to its former glory, but faithless vermin like Blaire are trying to stop Her plan." He shut his eyes as if in reverence to *Her*, whoever she was.

He pressed the button to stop at the next floor. "You will be the offering that gets me my snake eyes."

The door opened to reveal the robed figure standing there.

Morgan's stomach flip-flopped. "Oh shit."

The snakes slithered from under the hood, hissing to beat hell. Adrenaline and fear drove her to duck. Deadly fangs glided past her in a blur and bit into the security officer's throat. He dropped her gun and dissolved to ash, leaving a pool of scum on the floor. Morgan scrambled to the gun but couldn't get a bead on the robed figure before it retreated into the shadows.

Chapter Five - Who is the Fellowship?

Morgan frantically banged on the studio's glass door. The Uber driver who had driven her here sped off, despite having been told to wait. She pounded on the door again. There was no movement inside.

Remembering she had a key, she used it to get in. "Blaire?" she shouted into the darkness.

No reply. And no dog.

She must be walking Samson.

Morgan moved through the newsroom and into the back office where she slumped into the desk chair. Years as an investigative reporter hadn't prepared her for what had happened at the condo. Her body wouldn't stop trembling over the ordeal. She still couldn't wrap her mind around what she'd witnessed: the hooded figure, its snake eyes, and the death of the security officer. She was lucky she got out alive. Focusing on her breathing helped derail the horror show looping in her brain. She awkwardly slumped in the chair and let exhaustion put her to sleep.

***

Over the whine of the computer tower, sporadic faint chimes awoke her. She leaned forward, switched on the monitor, and saw Blaire had been logged on to a media site linked to #SaveOurCity. Each chime was a reply to the blog post Blaire had written: *"Who is the Fellowship?"* In the comment section, posters were tearing Blaire's op-ed apart.

@BeachNikDan: Dumb bitch! The

Fellowship is #savingourcity! Do you better research!

Grammar was not NikDan's forte.

@OldPort4Life: This fake news weirdo yuppie's opinion matters why?

@GuildGuru: The Guild of the Beach Rats is to blame for those disappearances. I've been telling anyone who will listen. Ask the locals with roots that go back four generations. It's always been the guild to blame. By the way, I hate having to create a profile just to leave a comment.

@ILiveHereToo: You're right guru! Anything from a low-level bike theft to a high profile murder, the guild has been behind it!

"Where's your proof?" Morgan muttered to the internet troll.

@OldPort4Life: You're as crazy as the **** who wrote the article!

The Blaire bashing went on for

pages, defending the Fellowship and blaming the Guild for the town's woes.

@KimMom86: Those little thugs, roaming around town at ungodly hours of the night should be locked up. Bet those disappearances would stop.

Morgan couldn't take reading anymore of this garbage. Her fingers trembled as she typed out a response, including a description on what she had experienced but leaving out the part about the figure's snake-eyes; she didn't want to sound crazy. She backed Blaire's take on the increase in crime, homelessness, and disappearances being linked to the Fellowship cultists. She highlighted the part in Blaire's article about how the Fellowship was buying up affordable housing, only to hike the rents beyond market value. Cost reduction was offered to the residents who could not afford the inflated rent, but only if they joined the *Fellowship of Her Lady by the Sea.*

Pausing before she hit the send button, she thought there was no point in commenting. Anyone who posted something sensible and true was rebuked by Fellowship faithful or conspiracy theorists.

She deleted the text and hit the power button on the monitor. Her reflection stared back at her from the blank screen. The trembling in her fingers had stopped, and her thoughts were a bit more fluid, though she still couldn't believe what had happened at the condo.

Suffering the ordeal without reward riled her even more.

I need to get those flash drives if we're ever going to stop the Fellowship. Where is Blaire, anyway?

She should be back by now.

The frantic sounds of scratching on glass came from the front of the studio. With her heart pumping dread, she rushed to investigate. It was Samson dragging his leash, but no Blaire.

She unlocked the door, quickly scooped up Samson, and just as quickly relocked the door. "Hey, buddy." She gave him the chew toy she found at the condo. He welcomed it eagerly into his maw, as if he had never expected to see it again. "Where's Blaire, buddy?"

He stopped chewing the toy and stared at her with sad eyes.

She figured the worst.

Morgan looked at the locked door and thought back to the comment section of Blaire's blog. Her social-media campaign was failing, taken over by the opposition. She needed to retrace old trails, develop new leads, and get her own sense of the curse on the city.

The Shovel and Bucket Café was her favorite hangout when she was younger, and as good as any place to start. Max's band had played their first concert there. Morgan had photographed the show and wrote a review that helped the venue and band gain prestige back in the days of Myspace.

***

Morgan walked down First Street, a block from the beach, heading toward what once was the boardwalk, alive with the thrum of music and the din of laughter. Now she didn't even recognize the beach.

As dawn broke, a shelf cloud on the far horizon blocked the rising sun's rays. The street was vacant going both ways for blocks. Samson walked beside her on his leash, quelling the lonely, empty feeling in her chest. What used to be sandbanks where honeysuckle hedges grew and beach shacks stood were now cluttered tracts of unfinished resort buildings twenty levels high, tarped and fenced off from the sidewalks. The construction sites, now clogged with windblown sand, appeared to have been dormant for a long time. The high-rises that were completed seemed nearly as vacant as the partially built ones, as only a few lights glowed from the hundreds of windows.

She stopped to let Samson pee on a weed.

A flickering headlight caught her attention, approaching swiftly in the unusual morning gloom. It was a golf cart loaded down with more kids than the cart seated. They were laughing and drinking from soda cans. Ropes fastened to the back bumper pulled four beach punks on skateboards, weaving between one another and performing tricks. One guy had a rat-tail dread and a slingshot in his back pocket.

Note to Mom. It's 5am. Do you know where your children are?

"Good morning." The teen driver showed her a peace sign. A little girl in a too-large D-A-R-E t-shirt was sitting backward on the bench seat, smiling at her.

Morgan waved as the cart whined past her. She felt giddy watching those clowns then walked in the direction of The Shovel and Bucket while Blaire's whereabouts again weighed heavily on her mind.

The once yellow café building had been repainted a sea-foam green and adorned in weathered wooden panels that gave the façade a rustic look. Faint strains of an electric techno beat filtered out from inside. The marquee sign read: *Aqua Lounge, Serving Brunch*, but worse, a biker-type brute sat on a stool in front of the entrance door. He sported a long beard, and his tattooed arms were folded across his barrel chest like he was some kind of bouncer.

She approached him with caution. "What happened to the Shovel and Bucket?" She pointed to the sign above the door.

The bouncer scoffed. "That shit-hole closed down years ago."

"What's a girl gotta do to get a scrambled egg around here?"

"Look, lady, this ain't no Denny's."

"The sign reads *Serving Brunch*."

"That ain't 'til eleven. For now, they got smoked salmon sushi burritos, or some shit like that."

Morgan crooked her eyebrows. "Doesn't sound very tempting."

"I don't make the menu."

"I guess it's better than going without breakfast." Morgan headed for the door with Samson in tow.

The bouncer blocked her with an extended arm. "No animals."

"He's my therapy dog, man."

The bouncer glanced down at Samson. "Don't look like no therapy dog to me."

"He keeps me calm whenever I feel like kicking the shit out of somebody."

His hard-ass expression softened to a smile. "Alright, but if anybody complains, I'm gonna throw you out." He lifted his arm like a draw bridge.

She gave him an appreciative nod and sailed past him and through the front door.

The Aqua Lounge smelled of salty

air and stale beer. Two college guys in beach shorts and their girlfriends in bikinis were playing pool in the back. Their bleary eyes told her they'd been partying all night. Music with no lyrics carried the strange aquatic sound-effect of gurgling water. Flat screen televisions on the walls flipped through images of marine life. A photo of a pair of angler fish mating in the inky depths was replaced by rolling waves over an underwater sandbar.

She took a stool at the bar where two patrons sat at opposite ends, staring into half empty beer mugs. Samson fitted himself beneath the stool.

"Morgan?" The apron-clad bartender approached her. His face seemed familiar. She thought back to her teen years and remembered him smiling at her in the school hallways, glancing at her from two desks away in English 101, and though they'd awkwardly exchanged cell phone numbers, she never responded to his texts, as she had been dating Max. But what was his name? "Chris?" she ventured.

"Awesome. You remember me."

"It's good to see a friendly face."

"Likewise. What can I get you to drink?"

"Orange juice. And I'll have one of those smoked salmon sushi wraps."

He waved a hand across the backbar and all his booze bottles lined up like good little soldiers. "With or without champagne?"

"With, please."

He prepared a flute of equal parts orange juice and champagne then topped it with a splash of Gran Marnier and an orange slice. "The food's going to take a bit. The cook has a hangover."

"I've waited all my life for a sushi burrito. What's a few more minutes?"

He placed the glass in front of her. "Damn, I haven't seen you since graduation. How's life as a big-shot journalist?"

He must have heard about her last story going bust. Now he was ready to rub her nose in it because she'd snubbed him when they were teens. "It didn't work out."

"Oh?" He tweaked his brows as if genuinely shocked. "That's too bad. I enjoyed reading your articles in the school paper."

She choked on her Mimosa. "I didn't know anyone read that drivel."

"So, are you back for the reunion show?"

"Say what?"

"Yesterday, some beach punks hung up a concert flyer for the Guild of the Beach Rats." He pointed past her to the wall near the entrance where a bulletin board hung.

"Concert, you say?" She hopped down from the stool to see for herself. Samson trotted behind her, dragging his leash. The band flyer resembled the cartoon-rats style she had used for the band in the past, back when she helped promote them. She tore the flyer down and brought it back to the bar.

Samson stopped to pee on a table leg.

"Told ya," Chris said.

She took another sip of her drink. "It can't be the original musicians."

"People are saying Max is back from surfing in Australia."

"Impossible," she muttered into her glass.

Max is dead.

"You gonna go? To the concert?"

"Nah." Without Max, what good could come of it. "I came back to help Blaire Hudson with a project."

"Haven't seen her in a while. I hear she doesn't get out much."

Well, she's out now and I don't know where.

Chapter Six - Prince of the Beach Rats

The *Dunes* was a heavily gated and privately secured ritzy beach community. Each house was a mansion with its own gate, polished driveway, and walls and greenery for privacy. The manor at *Ocean 6* was built into the limestone ridge and rose four stories above the sandbank. Due to the immense separation between neighbors, most residents believed the house to be vacant.

As Max ascended the sloping front lawn toward the manor, it hardly looked empty. A dune buggy, a few golf carts, bicycles, scooters, and skateboards were haphazardly parked or dropped along the circular drive. At the large double doors stood a guard, a barefoot and sunburnt punk playing a hand-held Nintendo. The kid opened the door for Max without looking up from the game's screen.

Inside the manor, children ran wildly, laughing. Kids slid down a spiraling staircase banister, shouting swear words from the third level of the house. Their unchecked joy echoed from the vaulted ceilings, their volume only matched by a television blasting an action cartoon from somewhere farther down one of the many mansion halls.

A little boy with a mane of dreads ran up to Max and grabbed his hand. "The Master is waiting for you." The boy guided him through the chaos, stepping over toys and dodging hide-and-seekers. He followed the boy into a room where the walls were lined with bookshelves that touched the ceiling. Punks sprawled haphazardly on a leather sofa, and some kids sat with their legs crossed in a circle around an older punk reading a fairytale from an ancient tome. The storyteller and his listeners didn't notice Max and his guide.

"In there." The boy pointed to a section of bookcase that had been levered open. Beyond the threshold lay limestone steps and chisel-hewed walls that dropped beneath the mansion.

"Wait." Max stopped the boy from running off. "Where does this lead?"

"To the sacred place," the boy said cheerfully and skipped out of the library.

Max descended the steps until the darkness became illuminated by torches burning along the walls of a cavern. Between gaps in stalagmites, he saw a lagoon in the center of the cave. A coral-reef island lay beyond the rocky shore. There the Master waited next to a decimated statue that stood in the middle of the island. A feeling of serenity overcame Max as he walked to the island on stepping stones that protruded just above the water's surface.

Max's gaze dropped to the reef he now walked on, mostly black and roughhewn coral. Miniature craters held puddles of water that reflected flickering light from the torches.

"What is this place?" Max asked the Master.

"This reef is very ancient and powerful, shown to me by an exiled Timucua shaman named Ethore. He taught me much of what I know."

Max looked closer at the coral sculpture that seemed to have grown out of the reef like a twisted tree. He noticed it was actually the towering body of an armless woman, and her head was shaved off, leaving only her shoulders and breasts on a snakish pedestal. He wondered who she was but asked a more pressing question. "What happened to Ethore?"

"A man known as the Priest and I studied under Ethore, but the Priest was seduced by *Guabancex*, the Mother of Storms. He murdered Ethore in Her name. I thought I had killed the Priest many moons ago, but now he has come back, and the more Fellowship followers he gains for *Guabancex*, the more powerful She grows."

Max felt a dead man's chill. "I think they're getting closer to the beaches. We destroyed a family of them earlier today, during one of their serpentine rituals."

The Master shook his head. "The

Fellowship's snake dances must not come close to the *Dunes* and this sacred reef. The Priest will restore this statue and give *Guabancex* power over both the land and the sea. The city will fall into ruin if we don't stop him."

"What about the authorities? Can we turn them on the Fellowship?"

"The city's loyal police force is depleted. Those who are on the payroll are outnumbered by officers who are Fellowship faithful. And now the mayor is with them. What is the status of your task?"

"The band is back together… well…except for our drummer, but he'll come around."

"Excellent."

"We practice tonight, and we'll be ready for the reunion concert, for sure. The word is getting out about the show. There's an excited buzz going around the beaches."

"My Beach Rats are all looking up to you, Max."

"Aren't we all Beach Rats?"

"Mine are special. I sacrificed them to the sea in Guabancex's name, that the town be spared from Her wrath."

A fire started to grow on his insides as Max became disturbed by what he was hearing. "I thought you were the good guy...but killing innocent kids..?" Max turned away, shaking his head in disgust. "That's unacceptable."

"My children were unwanted and abandoned. I've rewarded them with a new life by my side, loved and given true happiness in their perpetual youth. You've seen my mansion. You've seen how happy my children are there. They want for nothing. Besides, their sacrifices prevented the destruction of this city and saved countless lives."

Max remained quiet and stared at his reflection in the lagoon.

Does the end justify the means?

The Master broke the silence. "I no longer perform the sacrifices, not since Bright-Eyes. With her I made a mistake. She wasn't unwanted and unloved, as I had discovered too late to save her."

The name Bright-Eyes brought Max out of his mental stupor. "Why is she so familiar to me?"

"I've spared you that memory."

"Who are you to do such a thing?" Max's internal fire became an inferno.

The Master raised his hand at Max, extinguishing the anger and confusion boiling inside him. "Look."

The surface of the lagoon began to ripple. His reflection turned to a vision in the water, a mighty galleon cutting through the waves under full sail.

"I was a lot like you in my younger days, a rebel with an adventurous soul. I never wanted to be the Master of Thieves. I was a merchant mariner sailing under René Laudonnière toward the New World."

The image of a young and armor-clad swashbuckler standing beside a nobleman with a feathered hat and styled mustache appeared in the ripples.

"We were tasked with settling a colony in the name of our king, Charles IX. Timucua natives, in awe of our huge force dressed in lavish robes and shiny armor, fell to their knees in reverence to our arrival and offered us fruit in woven baskets as if we were gods.

The image flowed into the open gates of a log-walled fort built into the dunes.

"There was a rebellion in the camp, as intolerance of the *savages* bred violence, and the rebels began slaughtering our humble hosts. The Timucua tribe shut off supplies to our settlement and revolted."

Max watched the tribes-people attack their false idols. Fruit rotted in the sun and galleons went up in flames. The gates to the colony slammed shut, and the lagoon's surface roiled in scenes of war, death, and destruction.

"The Timucua were driven from their land."

When the water settled, the surface revealed a wild band of buccaneers, led by the Master, raiding ships on the open sea. Their galleon sailed under the skull and crossbones flag. On land, the men sawed swamp trees into logs, hammered wooden pegs into walls, and erected a town on the carcass of the old fort.

"Myself, along with a crew of men, built a safe haven from mercenaries and foreign navies, all hell-bent on collecting British bounties on our hides, but Guabancex sought revenge for our role in the decimation of Her faithful Timucua tribe."

The lagoon's water revealed hurricane-force winds that threw the ocean into high swells that inundated the town.

"She threw storm after storm at us. We had to rebuild and rebuild again, our safe haven constantly vulnerable to attack. I turned to Ethore, the Timucua shaman, for help, and through his knowledge, I made a pact with Guabancex, that She would spare the town, but only in exchange for its abandoned children.

To keep that pledge into the future, she made me the immortal Master of the Guild."

"So you can never be killed?"

"Never say never, Max. With the deal broken, the only way to stop Guabancex now is to stop the Priest and his Fellowship. The city's future rests in your hands." The Master lowered his arm.

The vision strewn across the lagoon evaporated, leaving the surface peaceful again.

Max turned away from his reflection and looked back to the Master. "I don't understand how our rock concert is going to prevent the Fellowship from completely infecting the city."

"Ethore will see to that. He has a plan to prevent the restoration and unveiling of Guabancex's statue, and he'll recruit a Beach Rat who is not amongst my dear children. Ethore will appear to her in a dream and show her a vision of past events, a revelation, you might say."

"Who is she?"

"I've spared you that memory, as well. In due time, I will reveal her to you." The Master set a hand on Max's shoulder. "If anything happens to me, Max, my Beach Rats will follow you, wherever you go."

"Why me?"

"You'll see." He untied the lace of his necklace and placed it in Max's hand. "This is a jeweled eye from Guabancex's stone head, now lying at the bottom of this lagoon. The Priest has the other. It holds the history and memories of all our past events for you to carry forward without me. However, there is a danger here. It's also a conduit for life's energy if returned to Her stone head's eye sockets. Do not let the Priest get his hands on it."

Max lifted the fractured jeweled eye to examine it. Its iris shimmered the color of amethyst then changed to black as if it were looking back at him, judging him for the task to come. If he were alive, it would have scared him to death.

Not sure he was ready to wield such power around his neck, he stuffed the necklace into his pant pocket where it would be safe from the Priest's prying eyes.

The Master reached behind his sash and retrieved the sheathed blade. "This is a ceremonial knife. You'll know what to do with it when the moment reveals itself." He flipped it in his hand, facing the hilt at Max.

"What's so special about it?"

"In your hands only, it has the power of life and death over all immortals. You will need it should you come face-to-face with Guabancex."

He accepted the knife. It had a dull forged blade, a grip of decorated bone, and a small cross-guard. Though he doubted he could ever use the knife to kill anyone, immortal or otherwise, he knelt to push it inside his high-top sneaker then rose and bowed to the Master.

"Now go and carry out your task."

Max, spellbound by the Master's plan to save the city, turned to the stepping stones, walked across the lagoon, then followed the sandy path to the stairs. He ascended through the torchlight until he emerged from the bookcase and stepped into the sunlight pouring in through the library windows.

The children kneeled and bowed their heads to Max.

Standing straight and tall, he

moved through the mansion where the other Beach Rats stopped playing and fell silent in reverence to him.

Outside in the circle drive, Rat-Tail and Bright-Eyes stood by a golf cart and saluted.

"What's that all about?" Max asked, approaching the two teens.

Bright-Eyes bowed. "We hear you've been anointed the Prince of the Beach Rats."

Chapter Seven - The Priest

Blaire was forced through double doors, guided by her captors at either arm. Her hands were tied behind her back, and her mouth was gagged. Her head had been covered with a sack, so she had no idea where her captors had taken her. She knew it was the Fellowship who had grabbed her off the street while she was walking Samson. If it weren't for him and her concern for his safety, she would have fought harder when they captured her. The last she saw of him, he was dragging his leash as he ran back toward the studio.

Finally, they untied her hands, pulled off her veil, and removed the gag. She stood in a Christian church transformed to a place of worship for the Fellowship of Her Lady by the Sea. The symbol of a snake, coiled within the eye of a hurricane, was embroidered on black drapes hanging from the rafters. In the pews sat hooded Fellowship faithful, and in the back stood members with black bands tied around their right arms. In front of her and the congregation stood a platform and podium.

"Welcome," a man standing at the podium said to her. He wore a white robe, and his eyes were blindfolded with a white bandanna. "I am *the Priest.*"

Blaire turned to escape down the aisle toward the exit, but a hooded Fellowship thug blocked her and pushed her back to the platform. She stumbled and fell to her knees, sobbing and mumbling, "Okay. I'll retract my blog post."

"Do not be afraid, Blaire Hudson. This is a time to rejoice. You have been brought here to be converted. Washed of your sins."

"No. I won't convert," she cried out.

"You have no choice." The Priest began to untie his bandanna, and as he did, the audience began hissing.

From the Priest's uncovered eyes burst serpents that spiraled upward and then hurtled down toward a completely terror-stricken Blaire. The snakes' fangs pierced her eye sockets with a hideous squish sound. She screamed and kicked in agony as the snakes lifted her into the air. The bodies of the serpents emitted a crackle of electricity, ceasing her cries and convulsing.

The conversion had begun.

The Priest channeled Guabancex's

power. Slowly, the snakes dislodged from her skull then recoiled back into the Priest's eyes. Fellowship members rushed to Blaire to catch her and keep her from falling to the floor. Her head hung low, and her body lay limp in their outstretched arms. They dressed her in a hooded robe and set her feet on the floor where she stood on her own strength. When she looked up, snakes rose from her eye sockets and slewed back and forth. The scene before her appeared distorted, as if she were looking through a lens, the Priest taller and leaner, the congregation stretching to infinity. All freewill escaped her, and the deaths of all non-believers consumed her every thought.

"Guabancex," she screamed.

The hooded congregation hissed in exhilaration.

Chapter Eight - Gun Club

The bell chimed above the hardware store's entrance door. Jeremy looked up from his backroom desk and the photographs at hand. He hoped his brother had come in, so he could show him that he'd cleared out all the generators, moved them into storage like Ryan had wanted. However, Jeremy knew Ryan's rule was to give him at least twelve hours to cool off after a fight, so the newcomer could not be his brother.

"I'll be right there," he shouted.

There was no reply and no bell-chime to indicate the customer had left.

Photos of him, his brother, and

Max laughing and loading band gear into a rickety van were laid out on top of his desk. Those were the days, and being reminded of them made his decision easy. He'd bring his drum kit to the practice spot tonight and help the band destroy the silence.

Excitedly, he stacked the photos and set them into an old shoebox covered in childhood stickers. He finished off the tall Budweiser, crushed the can, and threw it in the waste-bin where it joined the other cans of the consumed six-pack.

He exited the backroom to look for the customer. "Hello?" Footsteps came from the aisle between shelves of fishing gear, so he turned that direction. Through his hazy beer gaze, he made out a fire that had been started at the front of the store. Six cloaked Fellowship cultists ran down the aisle toward him.

"Bastards," he screamed, seeing his family's legacy go up in flames. He raced to the front counter where he reached under the cash register and pulled out a double-barreled shotgun. Raising it at his attackers, he pulled both triggers, blasting the two nearest cultists in their chests. Blood, bone, and flesh spackled the shelves, and the two snake-lovers hit the floor with a double thud.

Before he could reload, the other four jumped him. Two disarmed him while the other two grabbed his swinging arms. They yanked him over the counter and dragged him toward the flames that were eating away at the storefront displays of fishing gear and camping equipment.

Jeremy flailed, punched, kicked, and managed to knock one cultist into the fire. He stumbled about, his cloak ablaze, screeching in agony.

Jeremy noticed a police officer's uniform beneath the burning cloak.

He pushed back on the cultist who still had hold of his arm. The other two Fellowship pricks circled him as if waiting for an angle to strike. Beer and rage fueled his adrenaline, allowing him to overpower the cultist and send him hurtling backwards into his two Fellowship buddies. Their meeting of the minds started with a crack, and all three bit the dust but sprang back up like demons from Hell.

"Shit." Jeremy rushed down the aisle, escaping the flames, but not the cultists' murderous intent. He leaped over the back counter and barreled through the office, pulling down shelves of cleaning supplies as he ran, and ducked out the back exit where his truck was parked. He jumped in, started the engine, and pulled out his cell phone.

The cultists had fought past the barricade and were bolting toward the truck.

"Call Ryan," he commanded into his phone, and it started to dial as he floored the gas pedal.

Two cultists dove into the bed of the truck just as it careened out of the parking lot and onto the street. Engine roaring and tires squealing, he fought to control the fishtail while the cultists hung on and punched out the back window then began grabbing at him through the jagged opening. One got him by the throat, and the other reached for the steering wheel.

The call connected.

"Hey, Jeremy. Have you changed your mind? We're at the spot, setting up to practice. I brought your drums. Hardcore Freddy is here to set up a live feed."

Jeremy made a choking sound as he fought for air and tried to keep the truck going straight. "Ryan...help," he croaked out.

"What's going on?"

"They got me...the Fellowship." He could only mumble out the words. "Third Street, southbound...the Gun Lodge...let Bob know," he managed to say before the phone was knocked to the floorboard.

The cultists had squeezed half their bodies through the back window. They showed no concern for their own lives. One grabbed hold of the wheel and cranked it to the right, careening the truck into a light pole.

The punch of the air bag, the sound of crunching metal, and the smell of smoke was all Jeremy knew before slamming into unconsciousness.

***

The lodge had once been a banquet hall, but now it was filled with animal trophies: deer heads, antlers, and skins displayed on the walls and made into furniture.

Bob tested the ropes to make sure the knots were secure. One of the Fellowship cultists had survived the crash, and Ryan had brought the hooded demon to the Gun Lodge, along with his brother, Jeremy, bloody and unconscious.

"Come on, Bob," Ryan said. "How many times are you going to check those ropes?"

"As many damn times as I want." Bob straightened up and rested his hand on the gun holstered to his hip, next to a ridiculously large cell phone. "You just keep an eye on Jeremy."

"He isn't going anywhere." Ryan gestured like he was revealing something behind curtain number two.

His brother was laid out on a sofa near a ping-pong table.

"He's lucky to be alive with the way that truck and pole were twisted together." Ryan shook his head. "And how that one survived is even more of a miracle." He shivered while looking at the hooded cultist, bound in ropes to a chair at the center of the lodge. In fear of the low hisses from their captive, like snakes lying asleep, they left the cultist's hood on.

Ryan scowled at Bob. "Where's the rest of your gun club buddies?"

"I got a guy on the way, but a lot of them can't be reached on account of the coming storm. How about, where the hell is the fire department? The Police? What good are they?"

The cultist's head turned toward Bob as if disturbed by his rant. He stepped back. "What the hell?"

Ominous hisses grew in volume, and two serpents rose from the hood. One snake struck out and looped around Bob's body, binding his hand that was a moment late drawing the gun. The other snake burrowed into Bob's nostril and exited through an eye socket with a burst of blood and flesh.

Bob shrieked. His body went limp, and as he fell silent, the serpents slithered under him and kept him from falling to the floor. Their broad heads and beady eyes surveyed the room for their next victim.

Ryan leaped the couch Jeremy lay on, dodging a strike for his throat as he ducked under the ping-pong table.

The door swung open and another gun club member entered in a rush. "This better be necessary. There's a hurricane warning—"

The serpents coiled around the

guy's ankles, squirmed up his legs, and sunk their fangs into his thighs.

He screamed.

They flung him into the air like a ragdoll on a rope, smashing his body against the ceiling, and then slamming him to the floor. Bones snapped, silencing his screams before he turned to black ash.

A single gunshot rang out. The hissing ceased, and the serpents dissolved into vapor.

Ryan turned to see Jeremy sitting up on the couch. He'd drawn his firearm and put a bullet dead-center in the hood of the cultist's cloak.

The cultist slumped against the ropes, its head lolled back. The hood had been blown off, giving Jeremy and Ryan their first look at their assailant. They stared in disbelief.

It was Blaire Hudson.

Chapter Nine - Void Crossed Lovers

Morgan lay down on the sleeping bag on Blaire's office floor. It reeked of Samson and Blaire's body funk. She wasn't sure which was worse, but she was far too exhausted to care. With Samson curled in her arms, she slowly slipped into sleep.

A dream came to her, and the name Ethore resonated from the darkness. Rain poured out of the night sky, stinging her face and causing her to squint. A skull and crossbones flag flew from the mast above her. Beneath her feet, a wood-planked floor pitched and swayed. The roar of a storm and the crash of high waves shook her to her core.

Men in tunics rushed around her, fighting to keep their balance and shouting in French as they lugged heavy cannonballs across the deck.

The captain shouted, *"Steady as she goes."* His language was native to her ears. *"Man the port side cannons. The Conquistadors are firing on us."*

Flashes in the distance boomed louder than the thunder in the sky. A Spanish cannonball splashed in the ocean near the ship's hull. Another tore through the air past Morgan and struck a sailor, driving him into the darkness. The pirates unleashed a deafening barrage of cannon fire against the sinking Spanish galleon. Two more cannonballs struck the French vessel's hull, sending sailors and splinters of boat-wood flying. The deck shook violently and began to collapse inward.

"Abandon les ship," a scrabbling

sailor cried.

She dove over the gunwale and into the choppy cold depths of the ocean. A sailor's instinct took hold, and she swam to the surface. Floating on her back, she stared up at the sky, suddenly blotted out by a massive cloud. No. Not a cloud, a monstrous, jagged mountain that twisted upward from the waters, and a mighty hiss emanated from the mass, piercing the air like hell's own fury.

An enormous scaly appendage that looked like a serpent's tail arched up from the water, and then the naked body of a beautiful woman rose from the waves, a sight to behold until her face morphed into a broad viper's head.

A sailor bobbed up next to Morgan and screamed, "It's *Guabancex.*"

The Mother of Storms hissed, and Her fanged jaws clamped onto the

French vessel, lifted it out of the ocean, and snapped it in two. Ship debris, sailors, and stores fell to the water with such force that a tsunami rose up, washed over Morgan, and dragged her under.

***

The heat of the sun baked Morgan's face. Seagulls called out overhead, waking her to see a clear blue sky. The surf rushed in to lick her feet with tickling foam. She sat up on a sandy beach in time to see a Conquistador charging at her with a knife of bone and brass.

She jumped to her feet and lunged forward, shouting in French and barreling into the attacker as he swiped the blade. The Conquistador bowled into the sand, and she rolled away from him, barely ducking another slash. She had no idea she could be such a fighter. On her feet again, she noticed the Conquistador wore the robe of a priest under his armor. Preparing to defend herself with fists, teeth, and claws, she watched him regain his feet and brandish the blade. "You scuttled our galleon and for that you will die."

Out of nowhere came a tranquil singing voice. The siren's song calmed her with words she didn't understand. Pure notes drifted around her body like a gentle breeze, touching her mind with a sense of peace. She looked toward the Conquistador, and he too was overtaken by the same calming force. He lowered his blade and stared blankly down the beach as if searching for the source of such lovely strains.

Not of her own free will, she joined the Conquistador and walked at his side along the beach to the broken remains of an entrance to an old fort, nearly obscured in the dune. The Conquistador stripped off his armor, and now in his priestly robe, led her into a limestone tunnel. The daylight diminished the farther she strode, deeper into the sands as if in a trance, coaxed onward by the song. Darkness surrendered to an ethereal light that illuminated a great cavern where a lagoon pooled among ancient stalagmites.

At the center of the still waters lay an island reef alive with colorful coral that sprouted an intricate formation spiraling upward from its surface. Small puddles married and blended every hue and tone of a rainbow, all shimmering beneath a full-moon-like glow.

The formation's tendrils, like the arms of a reluctant lover, moved away from her touch, and the waters reflected her bewildered expression, not a reflection of herself...but of the Master's face, as she was seeing the dream from his point of view. His hair was lengthy and pulled back into a ponytail. He had soft blue eyes and a full sandy-colored beard. She wanted to run, but her feet wouldn't move, somehow steadfast on the island reef.

Behind the twisting formation, the source of the singing voice appeared, an angelic face on a serpent's body. The she-snake fell silent and slithered into the lagoon, quickly vanishing under the pristine surface.

The last thought the song instilled in her mind was to carve the twisted coral pillar in Her image.

The Conquistador priest, his face pale as bone, raised his knife to the formation, as if he too had the same thought.

"No," came a primal scream from

above, where a hut was built on a ledge of the cavern wall, overlooking the lagoon. There stood an elderly man, clothed in moss and animal hide, his dark arms heavily tattooed. He looked tall with his long gray hair wrapped in a mighty high bun.

"Who are you?" Morgan shouted, her deep voice echoing away.

"I am the shaman known as Ethore the Exiled."

"I know that name."

"You are the Master of Thieves. Your companion is the Priest, who even now conspires to destroy you."

"How?"

"See for yourself."

She looked back at the coral formation. The carving had been done. The beautiful tendrils that once waved magically and innocently were cut off. The Priest had shaped the spiraling formation into a giant serpent's body with a woman's naked torso, beautiful face, and long flowing hair. He'd inserted reptilian-shaped jewels for Her eyes. The shimmering array of hues from the coral island was suddenly lost, all faded to the grays and blacks of lava after it had cooled and hardened.

Morgan blinked and the dream shifted her point of view to that of her own. The Master and Priest now knelt like holy men before Ethore and the serpentine monolith with reptilian spangled eyes. She listened as the shaman explained how they were tricked into servitude by *Guabancex*, how they had unleashed an ancient power, borne of Timucuan lore, a power that would destroy the city with magic only the shaman fully fathomed. "And you dare to create a statue in her honor?"

Both men bowed their heads.

"With this blasphemous statue on our sacred island, there will be no stopping Her wrath and the flooding of this land." Ethore grabbed the Priest's knife and slashed off the serpent woman's stone head. The decapitation fell to the reef at his feet where he jammed the point of the blade into each of the statue's eyes and plucked them out. He unwound the bun of gray hair on his head, and with the knife, shaved off a fistful of locks, and then weaving them tightly together, he fashioned two necklaces, fastened one to each fractured eye, and hung them around the necks of the Priest and the Master. "I curse you both. Her vengeance is now yours to bear."

Morgan's perspective began to drift away from the lagoon. As she drew farther in reverse, the scene between the Shaman, the Priest, and the Master unfolded on one foggy stage, centered around the monolith. Phantom images of the three men performing rituals, humming tunes, and chanting prayers faded, and then materialized fluidly into the last act when the Priest pulled his knife out of Ethore's back, leaving him to fall to the base of the statue.

When the Priest turned the blade on the Master, a struggle ensued. The Master won the knife and stabbed the Priest's chest. He fell into the lagoon and sunk to the bottom. With the same knife, he hacked at the statue until the reptilian scales had been messily amputated. After the Master tossed the fragmented statue parts into the lagoon, where they sank, along with the eyeless head, he sheathed the knife and slipped it behind his sash.

Morgan's dream shifted again.

A flash of lightning revealed the serpent woman's form in the clouds. She found herself at the edge of a ridge where Max was barely hanging on. The ocean tossed violently below him. He reached up for her extended hand, but he could not grab it in time.

"Morgan," he screamed as he fell into the abyss.

***

Max awoke in a flailing frenzy, as if he were still battling the ocean's pull. On the television, a priest's voice preached: "This town is doomed. Pestilence and sin run rampant within the juvenile ranks of the Guild. There is hope. Guabancex is your salvation, my reverent brothers and sisters." A congregation off-screen applauded. "Join us tonight for the grand unveiling—"

Bright-Eyes turned off the TV. Rat-Tail opened the blinds. Clouds blocked the midday sun.

Max had not known they were standing guard over him. "What happened?"

"Enough about Morgan," Bright-Eyes squeaked out. "You're late to band practice."

"Morgan? Where did you hear that name?"

"You yelled it in your sleep." Bright-Eyes walked to the door. "You coming?"

His heart felt like it was pounding. He rubbed his chest. There was no heartbeat, but the feelings were there, panic and fear. The last thing he remembered of the dream, he was hanging on a ledge, reaching for Morgan's hand, and he screamed her name as he fell to the roiling ocean below.

He shook his head and tried to think clearly. The dream seemed so real, but as a memory, not so much.

The fractured eye vibrated in his pocket as if speaking to him.

Something else happened the night he died, he was sure of it.

And Morgan wasn't there.

Chapter Ten - The Practice Spot

Morgan woke from the nightmare that made no sense to her. The night of the storm had become a jumbled memory over the past ten years, a tragedy she had not witnessed, only felt. Max had fallen into the sea and drowned. She told everyone he had run off to surf the world. She thought for sure his body would wash ashore, but when it didn't, she kept telling the lie until people stopped asking about Max and she was long gone from the town.

However, Max had survived. The proof was in the flyer. The band was getting back together again.

The parts in the dream about the

Shaman, the Priest, and the Master rushed back to her. The history between those three was clear. Their conflicts were all connected to the Fellowship of Her Lady by the Sea. Somehow, Max was connected too.

Samson licked her face, reminding her to get up from the sleeping bag. As Morgan readied to take Samson out for his walk, Blaire's computer beeped. It came from a pop-up app. She sat at the desk as a video played without prompt.

A preacher in a black robe stood at a podium in front of a hooded audience of at least a thousand Fellowship members. A white silk sash was wrapped around his eyes. His skin was as pale as the Priest's in her dream. She remembered the lagoon...when he attacked the Master with a knife. It was the same priest; she was sure of it, though she distinctly remembered the Master stabbing him in the chest, and he sank into the lagoon. He couldn't be the same priest on TV now.

"Join us at the unveiling."

The video went blank and came back on with a cartoonish sketch of a rat holding a picket sign that read: *KEEP OFF DUNES.*

A live stream of a dude with a multicolored mohawk flickered on. "Forget the unveiling," he said. "Instead, join us for the reunion show to save our city. The Guild of the Beach Rats is fighting back, and we're tired of a twisted religion telling us we are the problem. Bring your instruments, your brass, wood, and strings, whatever makes noise, and come make music with us at the Beach Pavilion, tonight, at the same time the Fellowship unveils their goddess and tries to take over the town." He had to yell over the blasting decibels of a three-piece rock band playing in the background, surrounded by a bunch of Beach Rats moshing.

She then recognized the Mohawk guy; it was Hardcore Freddy. He oversaw the storage unit facility on Old Port Road. She remembered back to when the band would practice there, day and night. Sometimes he'd fill in on lead guitar, but mostly he was the tech guy. She stared hard at the screen, looking past Freddy's spiked hair to the background at the head of the band where Max sang into a microphone and played a synthesizer-keyboard.

"Beach Rats Never Die!"

Her next breath hitched in her throat. It was true. Max was alive. The impossible became possible. Why had her dream been so horrifically vivid, watching him fall to his death?

Max has a lot of explaining to do.

She phoned a ride-share and poured Samson more food than his bowl could hold...as if it were his last meal.

***

As the Uber driver neared the storage facility, Morgan gripped the inside door handle. She was ready to jump out as soon as the vehicle came to a stop.

"Hey, Miss," the driver said as he stopped the car. "I know there's a lot of fake news going around, but a town evacuation is pending. A big storm is sitting off the coast and headed this way. I got the alert on my phone a little while ago."

"I'm not going to run." She exited the vehicle and slammed the door.

As the driver sped away, she glanced around the storage facility's frontage. Beach Rat punks crowded the rooftops, bopping their heads to the hard rock beat of music playing from somewhere behind the walls that surrounded a labyrinth of storage units. Their beady eyes locked onto her approach. A few punks recorded her on outdated smartphones. *Tetris Storage,* the sign read above the steel-fenced gate. The company used to be called *You Pack It - We Store It.* Morgan reached for the call button on a speaker box next to the gate but stopped when the gate began to creak open.

A static noise emitted from the speaker before Freddy's voice broke through. "We're in the back. You know the spot."

The punks watched as she passed through the gate and it closed behind her. She retraced her steps from over ten years ago, and suddenly she was her teenaged self with journal and camera in hand, following the sound of Max's voice, which filled the corridors of the outdoor facility.

The air-slapping sound of a helicopter flying dangerously close to the rooftops brought her out of her giddy trance. Another police chopper followed.

The music stopped.

Frantic shouting echoed through the facility. A crash at the gate sounded like a car had wrecked. The walls shook. Morgan pressed herself against one of the storage unit doors.

Four punks sprinted past her in a rush to get away from the gate. "It's the Fellowship goons and the cops," the youths warned her as they fled.

An armored truck dragging gate rails tore after them.

The helicopter flew by again, and this time it dropped several grenades.

One clunked and bounced between the corridor walls, not far from where Morgan cowered in fear. A bang and flash rocked the alley between storage units. The flash made her vision turn all-white; the concussion threw her to the ground; the ringing in her ears faded along with all consciousness.

She awoke to blurred vision and the sense of jostling in motion. Someone was carrying her, running, darting and jogging this way and that. Her muffled hearing made out the sounds of sirens wailing, people shouting, screaming, gunshots, and the helicopter circling overhead.

"In there," someone said.

She heard a storage unit door roll up, through which she moved, and then the door rolled down and slammed shut.

"Over here," someone said in the

darkness.

She was laid on a pallet of flattened boxes. Fighting to make sense of what had happened, she sat up. The dizziness eased, and her vision and hearing were coming around. She shook her head to clear the cobwebs. Someone flipped a switch, and a light bulb buzzed to life.

Two teenagers and Hardcore Freddy stood in front of her.

"That was too close." Freddy wore a jean vest with more band patches stitched into the fabric than she could count. His arms and neck looked like his vest, covered in self-inked tattoos of fading band logos. The roots of his multicolored Mohawk had been dyed green.

"Not sure how long the backup generator will hold. We need to get out of here." He looked around the unit. A pile of used clothing and a mountain of stacked boxes cluttered the space. An a-frame sign read: *Free clothes for the poor.*

The teenagers remained deathly still, staring at Morgan intently. One was a girl who had such an imposing presence, Morgan couldn't look away.

Freddy's panicked gaze returned to Morgan. "Damn, it's good to see you. You okay?"

She nodded, still trying to figure out how to thank Freddy for coming to her rescue. She got to her feet, wobbled a little.

"Morgan, I want you to meet Rat-Tail and Bright-Eyes. They're with the original Guild of the Beach Rats."

"Hello," she managed to say, a bit disappointed that they were just kids. "Now what do we do?"

"Reports are cops and Fellowship thugs are working together. They have the beaches under lockdown.

Guess us hijacking their news stream really pissed them off."

"They want to stop the concert," Bright-Eyes blurted out.

Outside, the sounds of gunfire and yelling raged on.

"We gotta get going." Rat-Tail moved to the door and bent to pull it up.

"Where's Max?" Morgan asked.

"He's heading for the old pier," Bright-Eyes said as if delivering an urgent message from the King. "He sent us to help get you there."

"It's stuck." Rat-tail strained on the door handle.

"Let me." Freddy nudged Rat-Tail aside and lifted the door just enough for him to squat down and peek underneath. The corridor appeared empty, except for tear gas lingering in the air.

"Looks like we can make a run for

it now," Freddy whispered, standing. Just after the words left his lips, he screamed. His chest bulged out and burst as a serpent emerged. Several more snakes slithered in from under the door. They entangled Freddy's legs, arms, and bit his face. Blood gurgled from his mouth as his body was jerked and bent beyond its normal shape, then pulled through the gap under the door.

Morgan, Bright-Eyes, and Rat-Tail had rushed to help Freddy, but terror had caused them to stop.

"Freddy. No. Not Freddy." Morgan fought back tears.

Bright-Eyes stared down at the bloodied ground but merely sighed, as if such horror was a normal occurrence in her life.

Rat-Tail shook his shock aside. As the helicopter thumped in the distance, he pulled a leather bag from his pocket and dumped the contents on the top of a cardboard box. Pogs spilled out: small, circular, multi-colored metallic discs, painted with shimmering holographic skulls and daggers and lightning bolt designs. A shiny flying saucer-shaped pog was the last to fall from the bag and clunk onto the pile.

Rat-Tail snatched up the saucer, pulled the slingshot from his back pocket, and loaded the pog into the leather projectile pouch.

"That's your lucky Slammer," Bright-Eyes proclaimed.

"I'm going to cause a distraction so you guys can get away." Rat-Tail yanked up the door completely and jumped out into the corridor. At the far end, between two rows of storage units, a group of hooded cultists and uniformed cops had gathered. The cultists circled around Freddy's body and stomped and kicked him while the cops stood idly by and watched the mauling. None of them had noticed the boy and his slingshot.

The helicopter swooped in low for another flyover, close enough to the units' rooftops that Rat-Tail could see the smirk on the pilot's face as he glared down at the havoc he'd helped create.

Rat-Tail drew back the Slammer, stretching the rubber pulls and aiming at a spot in the sky where the helicopter was headed. When the rubber pulls felt like they were going to snap from the tension, Rat-Tail let the Slammer go soaring. It shrieked through the air until it pierced the windshield and wedged into the pilot's face.

The helicopter nose-dived into a parking lot across the street from Tetris Storage and exploded into a mushroom cloud of fire and smoke. Cultists and cops stood frozen in place as they stared at the hellish spectacle.

Rat-Tail whooped and hollered in victorious joy.

His antics got the attention of the thoroughly pissed-off-looking police. They charged toward him with guns blazing.

He dashed down the corridor in the opposite direction of the exit.

Bright-Eyes took Morgan by the hand, and they ran for their lives.

Chapter Eleven - Lover's Post

Morgan and Bright-Eyes joined the other youths fleeing the practice spot. They had lost Rat-Tail, as the bulk of the cultists and cops had chased after him.

In small groups, the Beach Rats broke away to escape capture, some taking off down the backstreets of darkened suburban subdivisions and the trashy trailer-park-lots of Oldport. Others vanished into the acres of swampy wilderness that separated the subdivisions from the vacant and graffitied strip-malls along the beach roads.

Bright-Eyes stopped under a light pole as the sun fell to the west. In the opposite direction, angry gray clouds swirled across the horizon and darkened as they approached land. Lightning without thunder flashed in the sky, and when it was brightest, Guabancex's eye appeared in the maelstrom, glaring down at the beach-side city with an ancient and malicious stare. The eye reminded Morgan of the dream with Ethore and his knife assault on the stone head.

The entire neighborhood sizzled with an unseen energy to the point the streetlamp's buzz was amplified and likely to blow. Morgan could feel the power in her chest despite her heart still pumping with adrenaline and dread. She realized she was still holding Bright-Eyes' hand and gently let it go. "Did you see that?"

Bright-Eyes hadn't been paying attention. She was studying the street pole cluttered with surf and skate stickers. At the top of the pole, she spotted a stenciled graffiti, a rat holding a picket sign reading: *KEEP OFF DUNES.* "This is it." She flopped down on the street curb.

The night was filling with the storm's ferocity.

Morgan took a seat next to the girl on the curb. She extended her legs, placing the heels of her beat-up Converses into the empty street. It felt good to stretch her legs, but she felt sad that Blaire wasn't with her, and Freddy and Rat-Tail, too.

"Is someone coming for us?"

"Rat-Tail will be here. That's the sign I look for when I'm lost or in trouble." Bright-Eyes pointed to the top of the light pole where the rat held the picket sign.

Morgan nodded, not wanting to tell her Rat-Tail was likely arrested or killed. She let her gaze drift up to the ominous clouds stacking along the horizon. Despite the chaos circling, her mind went to meeting Max at the pier. "I haven't been near the pier since it washed away," Morgan said, sharing her thought with the girl.

Bright-Eyes gave her a long stare. "You're cooler than I first thought. I see why he chose you."

Morgan looked at the little girl sideways.

How does she know that we were a couple?

A beat-up dune buggy honked from down the street. The horn was a silly ice-cream-truck type melody that lasted longer than necessary. She imagined Fellowship thugs running from darkened city corners like children on a summer day to buy a popsicle, only these guys had knives and clubs.

The buggy's dents and rust were

covered up in beach and band graffiti. Hitched to the back of the buggy, a trailer hauled band equipment. In the driver's seat sat Rat-Tail, smirking as he pulled up to a stop. "You need a lift?"

Morgan stood and rushed to Rat-Tail. "Lift your ass up. I'm driving," she said with authority.

He instantly complied, like a good son would mind his mother, and slid over to the passenger seat. "What's up with her?" he asked Bright-Eyes as she hopped onto the back seat.

She only shrugged.

Morgan glared at Rat-Tail. "I want to know how you could be alive."

"I led the killers on a wild rat chase through the storage facility." He laughed. "They're not so smart."

"Beach Rats never die," Bright-Eyes sang.

Morgan frowned, unmoved by the

lyrics from one of the band's songs. Now she focused on confronting Max to find out why he too was alive, and he'd better tell her a story she'd believe.

After making sure everyone was seated securely, she sped off toward the pier. Remembering what Bright-Eyes said about Max choosing her, Morgan glanced back at the girl who was gazing at her with a childish look, as if she was holding back laughter from an inside joke.

This kid is wise beyond her years.

***

Max stood ten feet off the sand on a busted and leaning lifeguard chair that hadn't been used in a decade. Its legs were partially buried in the dune, so he had to balance himself as if he were on a surfboard. He stared out at the storm that sprawled along the horizon, rolling the ocean into sadistic and dark swells. The wind flung mist from the crests as the waves crashed to shore.

She's here.

His instincts told him to run to the parking lot, mostly reclaimed by the dunes that separated the beach from First Street. He spotted the lights of a dune buggy dogging the sandy path toward the old-pier. Max felt a flutter in his dead heart, like he was meeting Morgan for their first date. He leapt from the canted chair and raced up the dune where he stopped at the apex to watch Morgan climb.

***

Morgan waved goodbye to Bright-Eyes, who stared at her out the back of the receding buggy. Rat-Tail had said he was going to the pavilion to help set up the band equipment for the show. Seems there was no rest for a Beach Rat.

She headed for the dune that she'd have to climb to get to the beach. The moon offered no guiding light, buried behind the clouds. Only the streetlamp glow behind her lit the way.

Wind-driven sand swirled down the dune and forced her to squeeze her eyes shut. A happy thought, that the rain had yet to fall, was muted by the nervousness of seeing Max again. When the blast of sand let up, she began her ascent.

Flashes of lightning cracked the sky, and she saw the silhouette of a dark figure standing atop the dune. It appeared in a flash, and then it was gone. "Max. Is that you?"

Max slid down the dune to position himself behind Morgan, who was still chasing his shadow with her gaze.

"Hello, Morgan." His voice circled

her like the wind and gave her a chill.

"Max?" She twirled around, mildly amused with his adolescent antics, but she refused to show him any hint of a smile. "You're supposed to be dead."

With a boyish smirk, he held open his arms for a hug.

Morgan could not refuse and welcomed his embrace, but right away she noticed his body felt cold, as if the wind had penetrated to his bones.

"I missed you," he whispered in her ear.

She resisted admitting the same. "I need answers, Max." She pushed herself out of his arms. "Where have you been?"

"Come on, Morgan. Follow me." He stepped around her and started to climb the dune.

"Max, wait."

He stopped and offered his hand.

She grabbed it, and they climbed the incline together. His cold and clammy hand caused her alarm, but she persevered. She didn't do well climbing the dune. The loose sand sucked the energy from her legs as she struggled with every sinking step.

Finally reaching the top of the windy crest, Max released her hand. "Race you to the beach." He slid down the dune and ran to the shoreline.

Morgan stagger-stepped behind him, not interested in his macho games.

"Come on."

A short distance down-shore, a small campfire glowed and flickered as it fought off the wind and rain that had just started to fall. In silence, Morgan trekked alongside him, dodging seafoam surging along the beach. Being next to him felt like they were two heavenly bodies sharing atmospheres as they crossed paths on their orbits, once every eon.

At the campfire, Max sat on a branch of driftwood and looked up at Morgan. "Sit with me."

She glanced at the firelight dancing off the dunes and the splintered pillars of the ruined jetty standing next to her.

"You recognize this place?" Max asked.

She ran her hand over one of the wooden beams. "Yes. It's Lovers' Post."

The letters M&M with a heart surrounding them should have been worn away like other coupled initials, now barely visible after years of weathering.

Adolescent romance. What's the point? It all fades away with time.

She remembered lying under the pier, staring up at the stars through cracks in the boards, cuddling with Max and being in love so long ago. She turned to face Max, his still-youthful face awash with firelight. "While this is all so sweet, Max, I'm done with this nostalgic nightmare. Hardcore Freddy is dead. Blaire is most likely dead, too." Just saying that aloud made her blood boil. "And you. What happened to you ten years ago?" Morgan's rant was nearly drowned out by the breaking waves and the rumbling thunder of the oncoming hurricane. She flopped her butt in the sand, feeling emotionally spent, more so than physically. The hot adrenaline in her blood began to cool.

Max watched her sulk beyond the flames. "I'm not sure what happened. Everything went black."

The wind and the ocean's roar were all they could hear while they sat, apart, in silence.

As the flames began to dwindle, Morgan made a confession. "I'm mad that I lied so many times about what happened that night. Now I hardly remember the truth. It's like it never happened."

Max moved from the log, around the fire, and knelt in front of her. "Something powerful happened, and a magic I have grown familiar with is keeping our memories from us." He placed his palms on her temples, cradling her head in those cold, dead hands. "I think I have something that can break the spell."

She thought he was about to kiss her and prepared to pull away.

Instead, he closed his eyes. "Shut your eyes, Morgan."

She did as he'd asked and felt him

inch closer to her.

He removed his hands from her head and took her hands in his, palms meeting and cold fingers interlocking with hers.

She felt something solid between their palms, like a rock of some kind. As much as she wanted to see what it was, she resisted the urge, so as not to break his concentration.

With the storm's fury bearing down on them, he whispered, "Now think back to the night ten years ago."

Chapter Twelve - The Truth

Torrents dumped from the sky in a blinding rage. The rain pummeled Morgan's windshield so hard that the high setting on the wipers couldn't keep up with the downpour. She drove into the pier parking lot and parked uphill in an area not flooded.

From the radio speakers, between lightning-induced static, a breaking news update announced, *"Hurricane advisory. Evacuation of zones A and B have commenced."*

She turned off the radio. "Why did you bring me out here, Max?"

He was quiet, staring out the window at the dunes. She had never seen him like this before.

"Are you upset that I'm going off to college? You and your band will go on tour. I'll come to your concerts when I can, and we'll see each other for the holidays. We can make it work."

"I know, Morgan. It's not that."

"Then why are we out here when we should be at the evacuation center. Do you have a death wish?"

"It's my sister."

"You have a sister?"

"When I was thirteen, she was seven years old. After our parents died in that car crash, she stopped speaking. Their deaths traumatized her to the point I couldn't take care of her, much less myself. The state committed her to a mental hospital. I was blessed when Jeremy and Ryan's dad took me in."

"I can't believe you never told me about her."

"I wanted to, but her story is so sad I couldn't bear repeating it."

"Is she okay?"

"She went missing a month ago. From the hospital."

"Oh my God. I'm so sorry."

"I dreamt that she's here."

"Here? Now?"

"She was kidnapped. I dreamt the kidnapper brought her out here for some kind of strange ceremony. Something evil is going on around here."

"It was just a dream, Max. You're overreacting."

"I'm going to look for her. Don't follow me. I have to do this alone." He opened the car door and let in the rain. "Thanks for the ride." He closed the door and ran into the tempest.

She had no time to protest, opened her door, and pursued him up the rain-soaked dune.

Max climbed to the highest point where the storm was blocked out by a dome of energy that sheltered a group of Beach Rats. Max stepped out of the rain and under the umbrella of energy. It was dry and tranquil within the dome, and the storm sounded distant and tame.

When Morgan reached the top, she attempted to duck under the dome, but it shocked her backwards, and she tumbled to the bottom of the dune. Her last sight was that of the dune rising like a titan's claw reaching up from hell into the sky.

Max's sister stood at the edge of the ridge, her eyes a blank stare. The drop-off behind her loomed above the raging ocean.

Rat-Tail stood back from the dangerous cliff.

"Bright-Eyes. It's me. Max. Come here."

She did not move.

"Come to me."

The Master of the Guild stepped out of the shadows, held out his hand to her, and forced her to take a step backward, now closer to the edge.

Max rushed toward Bright-Eyes.

The Master forced her to take the last step into the abyss, but Max grabbed her wrist just as she fell over the edge. She grabbed Max's hand with both of her hands and looked up at him with the eyes of their mother.

Max laid flat on the sand. "I've got you."

"You were never there for me before," she cried, dangling above the angry waves. "You left me in that hospital, but the Master set me free."

She'd stunned him with words, for the first time since their parents died. "You can speak."

"Pull me up."

The sand beneath him gave way, and the raging sea rushed up to greet him. At the moment he hit the water, a small body splashed beside him. He could tell it was the body of a child. A lightning bolt struck the ocean and illuminated the child sinking beside him. It was Bright-Eyes.

"No." He kept sinking, deeper and deeper, until he floated weightlessly and saw only black.

"Bright-Eyes," he called out in the darkness. Only bubbles escaped his mouth. His lungs filled with water; he knew he was drowning. His chest collapsed under the crushing pressure of the deep water where his body struck the seabed to lay among the creatures that would strip his bones of all human flesh while the storm tossed the ocean above him.

"This is me in my final moments as I settled into my death," he told

Morgan. *"I remember it all now."*

"You did drown...but now you're here. I don't see how you did it."

The fractured eye of Guabancex felt warm in his hand and pulsed as if it had a heartbeat of its own.

On death's lonely plain, a pale shimmer broke through the abyss. It glowed brighter as it neared. Angelic radiance emanated from a beautiful woman's face that floated just beyond Max's reach.

"Who is she," Morgan asked.

"It's Guabancex, the Mother of Storms."

The face swam close enough to kiss his lips. Another flash of lightning lit the murky depths, revealing the woman's body, the giant tail of a serpent. It twisted among children's corpses floating in the deep waters, from the beaches and beyond, to points Max and Morgan could not see from their dreamscape perspective.

Now the Mother of Storms broke through the veil of their trances and glared at both void-crossed lovers. "This is how the Master's city will die, drowned by my storm and blown to the wind."

Guabancex's siren voice made bubbles in the water, and as she opened her mouth, her beautiful lips morphed into a snake's deadly maw. She swooped down over Bright-Eyes and devoured her in a single swallow.

Morgan jumped out of the trance, jerked her hands from Max's, and flailed in the sand as she fought to breathe; she felt as if she too were drowning or sliding down the snake's gullet.

Max tackled her to keep her from rolling into the fire.

"I'm dying," she cried.

"You're awake now. Breathe." Max

straddled her torso and pinned her shoulders down.

She gasped and coughed, inhaling large gasps of air.

"Morgan, you're safe."

When she calmed down, Max helped her to sit upright. One hand steadied her by the shoulder while the other rubbed her back. Her warm flesh made Max feel alive.

As the wind howled and the waves crashed to shore, she finally regained her bearings. "When you didn't come back down the dune, I assumed you had drowned. Everyone kept asking what had happened to you. I didn't know so I told them a happy lie."

"Surfing the Gold Coast." He chuckled. "That was a good one. I died trying to save my sister, but I failed."

"Don't blame yourself."

"I blame the war between the

Master and the Priest."

The rain was coming down in a hard drizzle. Beach Rat adolescents were lounging on the shore and the dunes as if it were a sunny day. Bright-Eyes and Rat-Tail stood near the smoldering fire.

Max stood and threw an arm around Bright-Eye's shoulders. "This jeweled eye showed Morgan and me the truth about what happened that night."

"It's about time you remembered me." Bright-Eyes grinned at Max. "I was wondering when you would."

"I'm sorry I couldn't save you," Max uttered, his confident demeanor softening when he spoke to his sister. "And I'm sorry for leaving you behind after mom and dad died."

"It was meant to be, so the Master could save us."

"We're not saved, little sis. Our

being here is only temporary." He pocketed the fractured eye necklace.

Morgan grabbed Max's arm. "But the Master, maybe he can make it permanent."

"He used us. He's used all of you." Max swept a hand to Rat-Tail and the other kids scattered about the beach. "He's been sacrificing the town's children to Guabancex so Her violent storms won't destroy his precious city. But he stopped the sacrifices, reneged on the deal, and Guabancex is pissed. Turns out, the Master is no better than the Priest. We don't need them, but they need us to fight their battles."

"Max, please." Morgan let go of his arm. "Ask him. For us. So we can be together again."

"I'd like that, Morgan, but it's a fool's dream."

"Then let's be foolish."

"Ask for me too." Bright-Eyes hugged Max. "What's the worst he can do, say no? I need my brother, Max, now more than ever."

"I need you too, sis. I'll ask him."

Hope bloomed in Morgan's heart.

Suddenly, in Max's mind's eye, he saw a vision of The Priest with the Master. They stood at the foot of the reef's decapitated statue. The Master was bound to it with chains.

"Oh no. The Master is in trouble," he told Bright-Eyes. "I have to go."

"What about the concert?"

"We'll split up. Morgan and I will help the Master. You and Rat-Tail go to the pavilion and help prep for the concert. We'll meet you there."

Rat-Tail and Bright-Eyes shared doubtful glances as the rain came down harder.

Chapter Thirteen - The Master and The Priest

Arriving at the Master's mansion, Morgan and Max stopped at the driveway. Hooded Fellowship cultists were lined up at the double doors as if waiting to go in to see a movie. The downpour was now accompanied by a hard wind, which had no affect on the cultists.

Guabancex's full force was near at hand, but the last barrier remained, the Guild and their pesky Beach Rats.

Somehow, Max had to find a way to get inside. He dug the fragmented eye necklace from his pocket and slid it into Morgan's hand, then clutched palms with her and interlocked their fingers.

"What is it?" she whispered.

"The symbolic eye of *Guabancex*. We'll hold it and not reveal it. The Master told me I'd know what to do with it when the time came." His tone was hushed. "Maybe this is that time."

In unison, the hooded cultists chanted a hymn that sounded like meaningless moaning and hissing. Max led Morgan forward; the faithful were easy to maneuver through, as they were in a deep reverie.

The interior of the mansion had been cleared of the adolescents. The Beach Rats were at the pavilion, setting up for the concert. The Fellowship faithful continued their meditation while Max and Morgan moved through the mansion to the library. The hidden passage behind the bookcase was open. Together, and still clutching hands, he led her down the steps and into the dunes.

Standing between the ancient stalagmites, Fellowship onlookers watched the blindfolded Priest as Max and Morgan stepped within reach of the torchlights. At the center of the lagoon's coral island, the Master was chained to the desecrated statue of Guabancex. The Priest stood before him, triumphant, hands on his hips, while cultists pulled from the lagoon's depths the stone head of *Guabancex,* missing the eyes. More cultists waited atop ladders to receive the head and place it on the serpent's body, on which the carved scales had already been restored.

"Guabancex, you're as beautiful as ever." The Priest approached the stone head, holding the fractured eye he possessed and fitted it gently into the right socket. "There. Isn't that better?" He turned to the Master. "Now where's the eye Ethore gave you?"

The Master remained mute and glared at the Priest in total defiance.

The unveiling production halted. Two cultists placed the head at the foot of the ladder. The Priest slapped the Master. "Where is it?" He gripped the Master's face. "Perhaps, we can use one of your eyes instead."

The Master's eyes shifted to Max approaching the lagoon.

Max let go of Morgan's hand, leaving her with the jeweled eye, and hid her behind a stalagmite.

The Priest followed his old rival's gaze. "I see. Your flunky Max must have it." He removed his blindfold, and serpents lashed out like whips to wrap around each of Max's wrists. Yanked from the sandy path, he was thrown to the feet of the Master.

Several Fellowship followers broke from their ranks to swarm Max and hold him in place. The snakes retracted into the Priest's eye sockets and were again sealed behind the blindfold.

"Where is it, boy?" the Priest demanded.

"Go to hell," Max shouted. "This is the Beach Rat's city now."

"Your city isn't worth saving. It should not have ever existed, built on the bodies of the Timucua natives. My Fellowship rules now, in Guabancex's name. Seems your Master has failed to protect your city." The Priest patted Max down for the jeweled eye necklace. "Where is it?"

"This isn't my city anymore. I belong at the bottom of the sea."

"No, Max. No." Morgan abandoned her hiding spot and rushed to the shore of the lagoon. "You belong here with me."

The Priest turned his blinded eyes to her. "Ah...if it isn't your pretty little girlfriend. Perhaps I can persuade her to tell me where it is." The priest laughed maniacally.

"Leave her alone," Max shouted.

"Are you looking for this?" Morgan twirled the necklace on her right index finger.

"No, Morgan. Run," Max yelled.

She caught the eye in her left hand to stop the taunting twirl. The image of the M&M on Lovers' Post and the bygone aroma of honeysuckle hedges on the sandbanks flooded her mind. Gone were the days of the Shovel and Bucket and concerts on the beach. Rage that those things may never return to her home town fueled her courage and her disdain for the Fellowship and the Priest. "Let him go. And the Master too."

"Morgan, is it?" The Priest grinned wickedly. "Who do you think you are, coming in here all full of demands?"

"I'm a Beach Rat."

"You're a little old for a Beach Rat, don't you think?"

It was unnerving what he could see when he couldn't use his eyes, but she would not be deterred. "Beach Rats never die," she cried out and leapt from stepping stone to stepping stone, reached the statue's head, and crammed the fractured eye into its vacant socket.

"No," the Priest screamed. "The unveiling ritual is not for a Beach Rat to complete." He ripped off the blindfold, letting loose the snakes to make her pay with her life, but the damage had already been done. The snakes struck out but suddenly dissolved into a black vapor that filtered down through the coral at her feet.

The cultists holding Max exploded to ash. He pulled the knife from his sneaker, charged the Priest, and rammed the blade into his gut.

The Priest grimaced, his face a mask of surprise. He tried to say something but only croaked out his last breath. Max let him fall and watched his body turn to ash.

Behind him, the Master cried out, and Max turned in time to see his body dissolve and sift through the chains. It seemed as if the two were symbiotic organisms, good and evil, created with one purpose, dominance over the other, and now neither had won.

The headless *Guabancex* statue began to crack and chip away, raining down coral debris.

Morgan backed toward Max, and they clung to each other as the cavern shook and the walls crumbled. Stalactites broke from the ceiling and crashed to the ground, knocking stalagmites over like trees felled in a forest. Worse, the water in the lagoon began to rise at an alarming rate.

Max looked back to the way out, saw black piles of ash where the Fellowship onlookers had stood, and the stepping stones were now fully submerged. "Looks like were gonna have to swim."

Suddenly, the black reef was awash with brilliant colors as the reemerging corals shimmered and danced like something divine. And from this cosmic glory stepped the shaman, Ethore. He moved his hand over the Max and Morgan of Lovers' Post, and an air bubble formed, encapsulating them as the lagoon water rose and flooded the cavern.

Chapter Fourteen - The Concert

Rain fell from the sky without mercy. Chaotic dark clouds circled over the city. Lightning struck and the wind whipped unabated through the abandoned alleys and streets. In the distance, beyond the dunes and shoreline, the tidal surge had risen into a wall of water approaching with the roar and speed of a freight train. In spite of the danger, an excited crowd of fans had gathered at the canted beach pavilion to see the show.

"Hurry up," Beach Rat roadies shouted to one another as they positioned a ten-speaker system into place on either side of the stage.

Ryan plucked his guitar strings but got no sound from his amplifier. The Fellowship had shut off power to the beaches.

"Jeremy," he shouted into the wind. "How long before you get those generators working?" He pointed at the cluster of unboxed generators they'd pulled out of storage. Some were running while Beach Rats were fueling up others.

Jeremy was sorting wires and cords from one another, running cables to a multi-power distributor stationed under a canopy tarp strung down with ropes anchored to cement blocks. "I've almost got it."

The crowd had grown to over a thousand people, and they were chanting in unison an old line from the band's past. "Beach Rats Never Die."

Jeremy connected two cord plugs

together, and the sound of Ryan's guitar blasted from the stacked speakers. A bank of arc-lamps fired up, illuminating the stage. The crowd roared and the rain came down harder.

Bright-Eyes and Rat-Tail pulled the dune buggy up to the gazebo at the beach entrance, sounding off the ice-cream horn to signal their arrival. They were quickly surrounded by concert goers.

"We're with the band," Rat-Tail explained.

Bright-Eyes jumped out.

"Let them through." Ryan's voice boomed from the PA system. He tapped the microphone. "Testing. One two three. Testing."

The crowd parted. Bright-Eyes pressed to the front of the pavilion stage. Two fans helped her up to the platform. Jeremy had taken his seat at the drum kit and wielded his drumsticks like they were on fire. Ryan was strapped into his battle-axe and ready to slay. Max's keyboard and microphone stood unattended.

"Where's Max?" Jeremy asked.

"I thought he would be here by now." Bright-Eyes glanced around, worried.

"No lead singer? Not again." Ryan panicked, thinking of the time Max had abandoned them at the recording session ten years ago.

"We only have enough time for one song," Jeremy reminded them.

Boos started to bellow up from pockets in the crowd. Faces began to show fear of the mountain of water rolling in the distance.

Bright-Eyes looked up and pointed to the sky. "Here they come."

Max and Morgan descended out of the rainclouds, standing inside an air bubble.

The crowd's boos turned to *oohs* and *aahs*.

With Morgan by his side, Max guided their descent to touch down in front of his keyboard, and he spoke into his microphone. "In defiance of the Fellowship, this song goes out to you, our fans, and let it be the first song to bring music back to the beaches."

His voice excited the people who were attracted to him for the leader he was, bonding them in common cause and freedom for all. They cheered in thunderous agreement, pumping their fists and thrashing hips into one another.

Max touched the keys on the synthesizer, and an eerie electronic rock intro electrified the air, followed by the opening refrain to their most popular song:

♪"Beach Rats never die."♪

The crowd sang along and pushed back against the Fellowship cultists gathering at the perimeter to break up the concert.

♪"Born to fight. Destined to Rule."♪

The air bubble grew massive with each strain of music, expanding over the band and engulfing the crowd, but blocking out the angry Fellowship protesters.

♪"We'll fight, we'll fight. We'll win, we'll win. Beach Rats never die."♪

The mighty oncoming wave reflected the glare of the arc-lights, and looming in the maelstrom, a vision appeared on the water, the return of honeysuckle hedges in bloom, and Lovers' Post renewed and intact with M&M still carved beneath the renovated boardwalk pier, and the pavilion stage stood straight and white and sturdy again. That image shimmered before an ethereal sight rippled from deeper in the wave, that of the shaman as a boy with his father, rowing a canoe along a long-lost waterway, now vigilant over a city that had risen from despair.

The towering wave crashed over the beaches, washed the Fellowship cultists away, but spared those encapsulated in the shaman's magic bubble. As the water rushed back to sea, the bubble burst and dragged Max and Bright-Eyes from the beach.

"Morgan," he shouted. "Goodbye."

As he sank into the sea's dark depths, Bright-Eyes descended with him, hand-in-hand as before. Rat-Tail and the other Beach Rats followed their Prince down to their watery graves.

Morgan treaded turbulent water and watched the ocean swallow Max. Everything they were together and everything they could have been went down with him. *Guabancex* had demonstrated how fragile life could be in the eye of the storm. Morgan's heart felt empty, but she knew this story needed telling and retelling until the end of time.

A tiny whimper forced her to turn. It was Samson, doggy-paddling. He barked and swam to her waiting arms. With the city lights twinkling beyond the dunes, they found refuge on a busted speaker box, and together they waited for the sun to rise and the sky to clear.

There are some who believe a city has a soul, and some who think such things to be fantasy.

Morgan, she did not know, but she fully believed the Guild of the Beach Rats would never die.

Michael J.P. Whitmer

ABOUT THE AUTHOR

Michael J.P. Whitmer is a dad, husband, and speculative fiction writer living in his sunny hometown of Jacksonville Beach, FL. He won the Watty Awards Best in Horror 2010 for his story "Day of the Undead Sophomores" and 2016 Theme of Absence's Halloween Horror Fiction contest for "The Girl in the Window." His other fiction has been dotted throughout the web and can be found in print anthologies "UnCommon Lands," "See Through My Eyes," and "First Came Fear."

Michael J.P. Whitmer

Enjoy more short stories and novels by many talented authors at

www.twbpress.com

Science Fiction, Supernatural, Horror, Thrillers, Romance, and more

www.ingramcontent.com/pod-product-compliance
Lightning Source LLC
Chambersburg PA
CBHW060747180626
46818CB00002B/478